Sparky's Bark
El ladrido de Sparky

By Mimi Chapra · Illustrated by Viví Escrivá

KATHERINE TEGEN BOOKS
An Imprint of HarperCollins Publishers

Sparky's Bark
Text copyright © 2006 by Mimi Chapra
Illustrations copyright © 2006 by Viví Escrivá
Translation by Cristián Pietrapiana
Translation copyright © 2006 by HarperCollins Publishers Inc.
Manufactured in China. All rights reserved.
No part of this book may be used or reproduced in any manner whatsoever without written permission
except in the case of brief quotations embodied in critical articles and reviews.
For information address HarperCollins Children's Books,
a division of HarperCollins Publishers, 1350 Avenue of the Americas, New York, NY 10019.
www.harperchildrens.com

Library of Congress Cataloging-in-Publication Data
Chapra, Mimi.
    Sparky's bark = El ladrido de Sparky / by Mimi Chapra ; illustrated by Viví Escrivá.— 1st ed.
        p.   cm.
    Summary: When young Lucy travels from Latin America to visit relatives in Ohio, she is
very homesick until she realizes that the only way to communicate with her cousin's frisky
dog is to learn to speak English.
    ISBN-10: 0-06-053172-X—ISBN-10: 0-06-053173-8 (lib. bdg.)
    ISBN-13: 978-0-06-053172-0—ISBN-13: 978-0-06-053173-7 (lib. bdg.)
    [1. Homesickness—Fiction. 2. English language—Fiction. 3. Latin Americans—Fiction.
4. Dogs—Fiction. 5. Spanish language materials—Bilingual.] I. Title: Ladrido de Sparky.
II. Escrivá, Viví , ill. III. Title
PZ73.C45 2006
[E]—dc22   2004012411
                                                                                                              CIP
                                                                                                              AC

Typography by Jeanne L. Hogle
1 2 3 4 5 6 7 8 9 10
❖
First Edition

Dedicated to my encouraging Mother, Husband,
Ohio Cousins, and the memory of Sparky.
Special thanks to Katherine, Julie, and Kendra
for making this book possible.
—M.C.

For Paula and Juliete:
my two sweet and imaginative granddaughters
—V.E.

My excited voice rises above the noisy plane's roar and I beg Mamita to show me *"las fotos, por favor."*

"*Sí*," Mamita shouts. Holding up photos, she tells me about Papi's family, whom we're going to visit in Ohio.

Then THUMP, our plane bumps, rocking over the Atlantic, the sea of green. My heart goes CHA, CHA, CHA, until our plane wheels touch down at last.

Mi voz emocionada se eleva sobre los ruidosos gruñidos del avión y le ruego a Mamita que me muestre las fotos, "por favor".

"*Sí*," grita Mamita. Mostrándome las fotos, me habla de la familia de Papi, que vamos a visitar en Ohio.

Luego, ¡pum!, nuestro avión se sacude sobre el Atlántico, sobre un mar verde. Mi corazón late al ritmo del CHA, CHA, CHA, hasta que las ruedas del avión por fin tocan el suelo.

Mamita and I walk into the airport, and a man wearing overalls calls out, "Claudia, Lucy, over here." Without warning, he sweeps me into his arms and hugs me tight. When he finally lets go, he starts yelling, "HOW'R YOU?"

Mamita y yo caminamos hacia el aeropuerto y un hombre con traje de mecánico grita, "Claudia, Lucy, por aquí". Sin previo aviso, me alza en sus brazos y me abraza con fuerza. Cuando por fin me suelta, comienza a gritar, *"HOW'R YOU?"*

"*Ayyyyyyy!*" I cry, turning my face toward Mamita.
Softly, in Spanish, she whispers, "*Querida*, your American uncle, *Tío* John, is just asking how are you."

"¡Ayyyyyyy!" exclamo, y busco a Mamita.
Despacito y en español ella me susurra, "Querida, tu tío americano, tío John, te está preguntando como estás".

Outside, *Tío* John leads us to the parking lot.
"Here she is." He points to his red truck, *tan grande.*
It's so big, all three of us can sit in front.

Salimos del aeropuerto y el tío John nos lleva al estacionamiento.
"Aquí está". Señala su camioneta roja, tan grande.
Es tan grande, que los tres podemos sentarnos en la parte delantera.

On the ride to *Tío* John's, I stick my head out the window so I can see this new place. There are no banana groves in sight. No flamingos, no lagoons. I see only farm, cows, farm, cows, until *Tío* slows down, driving up to his white house.

En camino a la casa del tío John, asomo mi cabeza por la ventanilla para ver este nuevo lugar. No veo bananos por ningún lado. Tampoco veo flamencos o lagunas. Solamente veo granjas, vacas, más granjas y más vacas, hasta que tío aminora la marcha y se acerca a su casa blanca.

I smile when I recognize Aunt Dot and Cousin Robby
from the photos. Suddenly, a fuzzy dog comes running.
"That's Sparky." Robby points to the dog.

Me sonrío cuando reconozco por las fotos a la tía Dot y al primo
Robby. De repente, viene corriendo un perro peludo.
Robby señala al perro y dice, "¡Ése es Sparky!"

With a sniff and a slobber, Sparky licks my fingers.

"Sparky, *déjame*," I say, but he won't behave. Jumping higher, he covers my face with wet doggie kisses. "*Por favor*, Sparky," I say politely. But he jumps higher and higher, until Robby has to shout, "Down, Sparky!"

Sparky me huele, me babea y me lame los dedos.

"Sparky, déjame," le digo, pero no se comporta. Salta más alto, y cubre mi rostro de besos mojados. "Por favor, Sparky," exclamo muy amable, pero el perro salta cada vez más alto, hasta que Robby tiene que gritarle, "*Down*, Sparky!"

"*¡Sparky se porta mal!*" I tell Mamita.

"*Ay*, no, Sparky isn't a bad dog," Mamita explains. "He just doesn't know Spanish."

Waving good-bye to Sparky, I follow Robby and Mamita into the house so I can take a little siesta.

Mamita tells me that Sparky will wake me in time for supper.

"¡Sparky se porta mal!" le digo a Mamita.

"Ay, no, Sparky no es un perro malo," me explica Mamita. "Lo que pasa es que no entiende español".

Me despido de Sparky y entro a la casa con Robby y Mamita para dormir la siesta.

Mamita me dice que Sparky me despertará a la hora de la cena.

After a nap, I'm hungry for my first dinner in Ohio. Aunt Dot passes around shiny plates to everyone but me. Only I get a dish *especial*, with a Sparky dog painted right on it!

Después de la siesta, siento hambre y deseos de probar mi primera cena en Ohio. La tía Dot da platos brillantes a todo el mundo, menos a mí. A mí me da un plato especial, ¡con un dibujo de Sparky!

Aunt Dot serves mashed potatoes and crispy fried chicken. My meal tastes good, but my mouth doesn't tingle. I miss sizzling chicken and rice. Bright yellow *arroz con pollo.*

La tía Dot nos sirve puré de papas y pollo frito. Sabe bien, pero no siento picazón en la boca. Extraño el pollo caliente con arroz. El arroz con pollo amarillo.

I feed Sparky my leftovers. Then, *"ayyy,"* he licks my hand, and I remember gooey mango juice trickling between my fingers.

I speak very slowly. "¡Sparky, *d-é-j-a-m-e!*" But silly Sparky licks all ten of my toes. Why doesn't he know Spanish?

Le doy a Sparky las sobras de mi comida. Entonces, "ayyy," lame mis manos y recuerdo el jugo pegajoso de mango goteando entre mis dedos.

Hablo muy despacio. "¡Sparky, déjame!" Pero Sparky lame los dedos de mis pies. ¿Por qué no entiende español?

Aunt Dot asks me something in English.
Mama translates: "How's dinner?"
I start to say, *"Sabrosa,"* but Mamita breaks in.
"Mira, Lucy, try saying 'tasty.' It's the English word for *'sabrosa.'* "
My cheeks turn red. *"Sabrosa"* and "tasty" don't seem the same
to me. "Mmmmmm," I answer so Aunt Dot can understand me.

La tía Dot me pregunta algo en inglés.
Mamá traduce, "¿Cómo está la comida?"
Comienzo a decir, "Sabrosa," pero Mamita me interrumpe.
"Mira, Lucy, intenta decir *'tasty'*. Quiere decir 'sabrosa' en inglés".
Me sonrojo. *'Tasty'* y 'sabrosa' no parecen ser lo mismo.
"Mmmmmm," respondo para que la tía Dot me entienda.

To my surprise, Mama gives me a wink, and I remember what Robby called his sparkling drink. In a teeny voice, I ask for "yinyereil."

"Ginger ale?" Cousin Robby laughs.

Zoom, I fly out of the room. I'm stupid, he must think.

Para mi asombro, Mamá me guiña un ojo y recuerdo cómo Robby le dice a su bebida con burbujas. Con una voz pequeñita y muy suave, pido "yinyereil".

"Ginger ale?" dice el primo Robby riéndose.

¡Paf!, salgo corriendo del cuarto. Va a pensar que soy una estúpida.

Mama catches up to me and holds me close. "Lucy, *mija*, Robby wasn't making fun of you. Being in a new place is hard."

Shrugging my shoulders, I ask if I can play with Sparky all by myself.

Mamá me alcanza y me abraza. "Lucy, mija, Robby no se estaba burlando de ti. Es difícil adaptarse a un lugar nuevo".

Encojo mis hombros y le pregunto si puedo jugar con Sparky a solas.

Through the sea of corn I ride Sparky like a pony. Leaning in close, I whisper how I miss the sweet-smelling streets lined with stands of purple orchids. Sparky cocks his head. Maybe he does understand Spanish. He's *muy simpático.*

Me monto encima de Sparky como si fuera un poni y cabalgamos por un mar de maíz. Me recuesto sobre él y en voz baja le cuento cómo extraño las calles perfumadas con las orquídeas moradas. Sparky gira la cabeza. Quizás entienda algo de español, después de todo. Es muy simpático.

I tell Sparky how much I yearn for Marita, my best friend at home, and my eyes flood with tears. Sparky tries licking them away. More drops keep dripping, and Sparky shivers.

I want to tell Sparky I'm okay. I want to speak to Sparky in English so he'll understand. I'm crying because I don't know if I'll ever see Marita again!

Le digo a Sparky cuánto extraño a Marita, mi mejor amiga allá en casa, y mis ojos se llenan de lágrimas. Sparky trata de lamerlas. Caen más gotas y Sparky tiembla.

Quiero decirle a Sparky que estoy bien. Quisiera hablarle en inglés para que me entienda. ¡Lloro porque no sé si jamás veré a Marita otra vez!

Later, when Sparky and I return, Robby is waiting for me in the kitchen. Sad-eyed, he says something like "aboloyais" and offers me some cake.

"*Muchas gracias,*" I say.

Suddenly, I have this idea. I ask Mamita if Robby will teach me English. When Mamita asks Robby, he smiles at me and nods his head.

Más tarde, Sparky y yo regresamos a la casa, y Robby me está esperando en la cocina. Con ojos tristes, dice algo así como "aboloyais" y me ofrece una porción de pastel.

"*Muchas gracias,*" respondo.

De repente, se me ocurre una idea. Le pregunto a Mamita si Robby puede enseñarme a hablar inglés. Cuando Mamita le pregunta a Robby, éste me sonríe y asiente con la cabeza.

At first, I complain, *"Muy difícil."* Cousin Robby brings me a book with pictures that match the words. I like the hats and cats and bats.

Al principio me quejo, "Muy difícil". El primo Robby me trae un libro cuyos dibujos ilustran ciertas palabras. Me gustan los sombreros, los gatos y los bates.

I carry my book everywhere. To the duck pond, the haystack, the cow field. All summer long, I practice English with Robby. Finally, one day when the corn is tall, I'm ready for Sparky.

Llevo mi libro a todas partes. Lo llevo a la laguna donde están los patos, al granero y al prado con las vacas. Practico mi inglés con Robby durante todo el verano. Por fin, llega el día en que el maíz está muy alto y decido que ya estoy lista para Sparky.

Into the barn I go, shouting, "HOW'R YOU!" and Sparky comes running. I call, "Sit," and Sparky flops down. "Yes." I pat his head. "Now roll." Sparky rolls left. "Yes, yes," I say, scratching his belly. "Stand. Yes, yes, yes! Sparky, good dog!" Then Sparky barks, and I know he understands my English.

Entro al granero gritando, *"HOW'R YOU!"* y Sparky viene corriendo. Le digo *"sit,"* y Sparky se tira al suelo. *"Yes,"* y le acaricio la cabeza. *"Now roll,"* y Sparky rueda hacia la izquierda. *"Yes, yes,"* le digo mientras le rasco la panza. *"Stand. Yes, yes, yes! Sparky, good dog!"* Y entonces, Sparky comienza a ladrar y noto que entiende mi inglés.

In a flash, I'm on the porch. Everyone stops playing cards. Do they hear my heart skipping with joy?

"What's up? *¿Qué pasa?*" Mama asks.

Gulping the air, I answer in English. "I say 'sit,' and Sparky sits. I say 'Sparky, good dog!'"

Como un relámpago, llego a la galería. Todos dejan de jugar a las cartas. ¿Acaso oyen mi corazón latiendo de alegría?

"*What's up?* ¿Qué pasa?" pregunta Mamá.

Tragándome el aire, le contesto en inglés. *"I say 'sit,' and Sparky sits. I say, 'Sparky, good dog!'"*

Cousin Robby doesn't laugh at my accent.
"Bravo, Lucy," he cheers.
A smile bursts across my face, sweeter than gardenias.
Now I can speak English!

"Bravo, Lucy". Mi primo Robby no se burla de mi acento.
Una sonrisa dulce se dibuja en mi rostro, más dulce que las gardenias.
¡Ahora puedo hablar inglés!

28